A Short Collection of Horrible Fairy Tales

ANDREW BUCKLEY

For Those Who Prefer
a Not-So-Happily Ever After

CONTENTS

INTRODUCTION

Dearest Reader,

It appears you've stumbled upon a rather distasteful book full of horrid little stories designed to amuse and disturb you. Rest assured, you're not to blame. Likely you were taken in by the adorable creature on the cover, or perhaps you love a good fairy tale and mistook this book for one that might contain some.

As it happens, what you have here is a carefully curated collection of short fairy tales from the worlds of Thiside & Othaside. Othaside is likely the world you're sitting comfortably in right now, but you probably know it better as 'Earth'. Thiside is the world living just to the left of you, the one you can't see. The one you don't want to see.

If you're curious about these worlds and would like to learn more, I recommend you pick up a copy of STILTSKIN by Andrew Buckley. He's quite mad, but the book is a fantastic read.

Sincerely,

The Creature Currently Living Under Your Bed

1 THE FATEFUL PASSING OF GNIMROG THE GNOME

Once upon a time there was a gnome called Gnimrog. Gnimrog the gnome wasn't an especially bright shining star amongst his people. If you asked other gnomes what they thought of Gnimrog they'd immediately tell you that he was too tall. Being tall was not a good thing when you're a gnome. It meant you didn't fit into the standard gnome house and that gnome clothing wouldn't fit properly.

Your average gnome stands a little less than two feet in height but Gnimrog stood at least two and a half feet tall, and to make matters worse his head was unusually wide making the tall pointy hat that defines a gnome to sit awkwardly askew atop his head.

To other gnomes, the most irritating thing about Gnimrog was that he remained completely ignorant of everything, including the unusual nature of his own stature. His gnome tribe who lived on the outskirts of the Dark Forest in the land known only as 'Thiside' quickly grew tired of Gnimrog's ignorance and held a formal town meeting to discuss the matter.

"He's not right. In the head!" shouted Gnorris, a fat gnome with a fuzzy brown beard.

"He's too tall!" chirped Gnigel.

"His head's too big!" added Gnit.

"Yes, yes, we've been over this before," said Gnargurk, an old and feisty gnome and the elected leader of the gnome tribe of the Dark Forest. "We all acknowledge he remains ignorant of his short comings and causes trouble in the simplest of situations."

"Gnalvin and Gnerrick were almost eaten by a warzgurt the other day!" shouted Gnorris (who lacked the ability to speak in a normal tone of voice). "Gnimrog was supposed to keep watch of the area while the other two gathered firewood."

"And what happened?" asked Gnigel rhetorically.

"He decided to climb a tree. Because it looked like fun! Meanwhile Gnalvin almost lost his leg and Gnerrick lost control of his bladder," said Gnorris.

"He's too tall!" reaffirmed Gnigel.

"I was told there was going to be fruit pie?" interjected Gnimrog who was blissfully unaware that he was the subject of the town meeting he was currently interrupting. "Does anyone know where the fruit pie is?"

"See!!" shouted Gnorris in a way that indicated no further argument was necessary.

In actual fact it took no more argument from that point onwards as the decree was made that very night to banish Gnimrog from the tribe. Gnimrog didn't mind because he didn't really know what was going on and assumed he was going on a trip. In many ways he was obliviously excited about the whole thing.

****

Gnimrog had no idea where he was going. He ventured north for a while but lost interest at the border of the Beast's kingdom. Not long after he turned east, he was robbed of all his possessions by a group of angry fairies. Gnimrog never really knew what was happening and just thought they were being friendly. He travelled east until he reached the ruins of the Emerald City and completely failed to notice that the entire landscape was glowing green due to the luminescent rocks surrounding him. He then turned south until finally arriving at a beautiful and pristine beach. The beach wasn't frequented by locals as much as most would expect. This was partially due to its inhabitants whose peculiar tastes had caused the coastal piece of paradise to be given a rather distasteful name: The Beach of a Thousand Deaths. Unfortunately, Gnimrog was not privy to this simple yet most important of facts.

****

The sun was setting with a flourish beneath the horizon sending the final rays of the day's light skittering across the blue water as Gnimrog skipped his way across the sand. As darkness began to settle comfortably across the land, the gnome sat himself upon a rock and watched the waves gently lap across the beach.

"Hello," said a silken smooth voice.

Gnimrog casually looked around and came face to face with the owner of the voice. It was a beautiful naked woman.

Her bronzed skin shone in the pale moonlight and her long blonde hair hung seductively around her shoulders covering her more private bits. Only her top half was visible to the surprised gnome as she was leaning against the rock that Gnimrog was sitting upon.

"Oh, hello," said Gnimrog.

"You're a gnome, aren't you?" she almost sang.

"Yes, my name is Gnimrog. What's yours?"

"My name is Princess Lenora and this is my beach," she said and smiled.

Her voice was almost musical. It didn't just flow from

mouth to ear but rather it filled the air and consumed every molecule within it as if she could say absolutely anything and it would seem like a good idea at the time.

"I'm sorry, I didn't realize the beach belonged to anyone. I should be going anyway," said Gnimrog and stood to leave.

Princess Lenora looked hurt in much the same way a puppy dog would when told it was under no circumstances allowed to urinate on the living room floor.

"Please, don't go. It's rare I have company and it's such a beautiful night."

Gnimrog maintained his blatant ignorance by not acknowledging her request in the slightest. "Why are you naked?" he asked.

Lenora, who was not used to such directness and couldn't remember the last time she hadn't been listened to, looked at the gnome with confusion. "It is how I dress."

"Well, that's not right. It can't be how you dress because you're not dressed at all."

"I do not need worldly clothes," said Lenora regaining some of her composure. "As you can see, I am a mermaid." To prove the point, she raised her lower half which turned out to be a giant, dark green, fish's tail.

"Must be useful for swimming," said Gnimrog matter-of-factly.

Lenora raised a questioning eyebrow. "Do you not find me enchanting?" she asked.

"I like your hair," said Gnimrog and then quickly added, "but you smell like seaweed."

Mermaid's that exist in Thiside; real, actual, flesh and bone, mermaids, are very used to people doing exactly what they suggest. Hence the confusion felt by Lenora when Gnimrog not only failed to find her enchanting, but moments later said goodbye and began walking away down the beach. Having no experience being confronted with such obstacles, the princess of the mermaids of the Beach of a Thousand Deaths decided to try one last time.

"Oh, handsome gnome," she sang out with all her might, "you are a stately and noble creature and it would be an honor for me that you would stay here a while longer and keep my company. It would please me greatly if you would allow me to sing for you." And she let out a small sigh from the effort of it all.

Gnimrog didn't even turn around. He just raised a hand, waved, and said, "No thanks! I don't really enjoy singing." And he carried on along his merry way.

Had the world of Thiside contained camels, these last few moments would have acted as the last straw that rendered the aforementioned camel's back nigh on un-repairable. The Princess Lenora opened her mouth to its full extent, unhinged her jaw, and extended her razor-sharp fangs before letting out a shrill scream and launched herself from behind the rock, propelling herself toward Gnimrog the gnome with the utmost of speed.

Gnimrog, being the oblivious and ignorant fellow that he was, completely failed to notice when the extremely hungry mermaid princess slithered up behind him and bit off his head.

And no one lived happily ever after (except Princess Lenora who was no longer hungry).

The Moral of the Fairy Tale:

You should not be ignorant of the world and people that surround you. While ignorance may save you from the persuasive powers of mermaids, it will have absolutely no effect on them while they're eating you alive.

Or

Beware of mermaids. They eat people.

2 THE ABOMINABLE HOBBY OF YETI

Once upon a time in the world of Othaside (known to its monkey-like inhabitants as the planet earth) there lived a mysterious and misunderstood creature known as the Yeti. The Yeti stood eight feet tall and was covered from head to toe with dark shaggy hair that kept it warm in the winter and caused an unnecessary amount of sweating in the summer. Its claws were long and pointy and its fangs were sharp and gruesome looking. Its general appearance could be described as horrifying, the stuff of nightmares, the most terrifying thing you'd hope never to encounter . . . and so on.

The Yeti was a wanderer who stayed away from populated areas due to the terror its general appearance often induced and instead chose to live in areas of distinct wilderness. Undeterred by the elements, it ventured from the frozen arctic to the deepest African jungle seeking that which it could not find. Like all creatures it had simple goals in life; to eat and to sleep. But the Yeti being an ageless creature had also developed an unusual hobby that often went unfulfilled for centuries.

Several humans in Othaside took an interest in the strange creature while others discounted his very existence as being a myth. Occasionally a lucky traveler would catch a glimpse of the creature, but the pictures often turned out blurred or on certain occasions depicted nothing more than a large monkey or an unconventionally hairy human. The truth was that only three men had ever managed to get close enough to the Yeti to actually verify he even existed.

The first was Billy Eubanks, a child prodigy ballet dancer, turned store clerk, turned shoe salesman. After seven straight months of not selling even one shoe, let alone a pair, Billy decided to sell everything he had and go in search of the Yeti as it occurred to him that the chances of him finding an abominable snowman was a hell of a lot better than him selling a pair of shoes. As it turned out, Billy was completely right.

He traveled through the frozen wastelands of the Antarctic on a beautiful spring afternoon. He made the tragic and later fatal mistake of traveling alone on his expedition except for a team of sled dogs who dragged him across one glacier after another. After two weeks of nothing but snow, Billy's supplies ran out completely and so he turned to eating the dogs. Another two weeks passed before the remaining three dogs rebelled and ate Billy clean to the bone. While the dogs were busy tearing him apart, Billy, who was clinging onto consciousness, noticed a figure through the snow. The figure moved a little closer revealing itself to be the much sought-after Yeti. The large creature shook its head sadly, waved to Billy and then turned and tromped off into the blizzard. Billy's dogs were found at a research outpost two weeks later, very much alive and extremely well fed.

The second individual was David Smelnick, a 37-year-old man who had majored in theatre, minored in mime, and studied with the bohemian's in southern France all with the distinct goal of becoming the world's most amazing dramatic actor. Unfortunately, David had a rare virus that caused his right eye to twitch uncontrollably whenever it felt the urge to do so. After being laughed off every stage he ever occupied, after every girl he tried to approach had slapped him for suggesting something rude and unspoken simply by winking, he resigned to become a drunken hermit and moved to a tiny log cabin in deepest, darkest Alaska.

One chilly fall night, the Yeti knocked on David's door asking to borrow a cup of sugar. David opened the door, completely drunk, carried on a civil conversation about the weather and the state of the economy while he filled a cup full of sugar. He bid the Yeti farewell and that was that. David remembered nothing of the evening or the ten years before and after the incident—this is simply the blissful ignorance of failed, drunken, dramatic actors.

The third person to see the Yeti was none other than Sampson Sedgwick, a former pro-wrestler (who went by the wrestling name 'Sampson the Giant' due to his large stature), who after being expelled from the wrestling arena after a series of well publicized indiscretions involving various popular kitchen appliances, sought the counsel of a Himalayan guru. The guru advised Sampson that his essence was contaminated and that he should embark on a quest of spiritual realization and cleansing. Sampson being a complete fool set off that very same day and began his journey across all seven continents.

His general body mass and formidable size served him well as he trekked through some of the harshest terrain known to man or beast. It was three years to the day he'd began his pilgrimage that he found himself at the height of the Appalachian Mountains in North Eastern America. It was at the very height of these treacherous mountains that Sampson began to feel his essence might be feeling much cleaner. The clear mountain air filled his lungs and the sun shone brightly, cascading shadows across the range. He turned and came face to face with a very surprised-looking Yeti. Sampson's life flashed before his eyes. It wasn't very interesting.

The Yeti looked him up and down as if considering something carefully. Sampson prepared to fight for his life as the large creature raised its massive clawed hands, reached out . . . and swept the ex-wrestler up into a perfect ballroom dancing stance.

This wasn't what Sampson had expected. To further his surprise the Yeti began to lead him in what he thought was possibly the Tango. They danced around the mountain top clearing, promenading one way and then side stepping, swiveling and, at one point, dipping.

Sampson couldn't help but notice the Yeti was incredibly agile for a creature of its size. The dance finished with a flourish and the Yeti released its partner, patted him on the head, and disappeared into the trees that lined the mountain top.

Sampson returned to civilization shortly after with an extremely clean essence and a new-found love of dance. The Yeti, a creature with an eternal amount of time on its hands, continued its never-ending search for the perfect dance partner.

The Moral of the Fairy Tale:

Never judge a book by its cover or a Yeti by the size of its claws. Outward appearances can often be deceiving.

Or

The Yeti dances. You should too.

3 THE TERRIBLE TALE OF THE NEFARIOUS NYMPH

Once upon a time there lived a Nymph named Eve. Eve lived in a beautiful pristine pool beneath a waterfall comfortably nestled within a dense green forest which thrived and grew as if by magic. In actual fact it grew completely by magic. No matter what the season elsewhere, the area surrounding Eve's pool was always sunny and bright with colorful flowers and the greenest of leaves. The sparkling water cascaded from the high cliff above and splashed into the cool and welcoming pool below. The beauty of the place was negated only by its dark and horrific source. The area flourished and grew because of Eve's magical properties.

Nymph's are hideous creatures that can change their form and appearance to fit your wildest desires. They can naturally tap into the pleasure centers of their victim's brains before turning into an accurate depiction of whomever or whatever they most desired. They would use their unique abilities and wondrous promises to lure weary travelers into their pools. Then, and only then, would they reveal their true terrifying form, blinding their victims with absolute fear. It's at that point that Eve would rip out her victim's soul and consume it causing a magical transference of energy that sustained the waterfall, pool, and the surrounding forest.

This was not always the way of things. At one time the Nymphs had fed on love instead of fear ridden souls. Using their beauty and powers of persuasion they made men fall in love with them and they would siphon their emotions and love until they were depressed and empty. This was effective for quite some time until the Nymphs realized that scaring people was much easier, took less effort, and shortened the process exponentially.

Eve lured men on a weekly basis. She was over three hundred years old and had spent a lot of time practicing. She was very good at it.

One day, Eve was enjoying her pool, swimming back and forth, admiring the surrounding foliage and flowers, when she felt a nearby presence. A young peddler of shiny things named Simon had entered the forest looking for water as he was parched and tired and hadn't sold any shiny things in almost three weeks. He'd travelled the length and breadth of the land of Thiside and simply couldn't convince anyone to buy his wares.

Simon was dwelling upon his poor fortune and busy wondering how there could possibly be such a lush and green forest in the middle of nowhere when he stumbled across Eve's pool. He was so happy to find water that at first, he completely failed to notice the gorgeous naked blonde female who had seductively draped herself across the edge of the pool. He also failed to notice that she looked exactly like the type of woman that he most desired. The hair color was correct, she had that playful look that he liked, and she was correctly proportioned in all the right places.

"Hello, weary traveler," said Eve playfully.

Simon was frozen in place with a ridiculously stunned look on his face. For a moment he began to think that his luck was finally changing for the better.

"Why don't you come over and sit by me?" she crooned softly.

Simon staggered his way over in disbelief. Disbelief was quickly suspended when Eve revealed her true form which was ghastly and beyond description. Simon made a quick transition from lustful and overjoyed to terrified and wetting himself in a matter of seconds.

With the speed and ferocity of an exceedingly quick mongoose, the Nymph ripped the soul from Simon's body and consumed it instantly. The body of Simon the peddler of shiny things quickly decomposed, rotting, and then drying instantly before blowing away as nothing but dust and a memory on a passing breeze.

Eve licked her lips, letting the magic flow from her into the surrounding forest and all was as it should be in the world of a Nymph.

It wasn't until four weeks and seven victims later that an Ogre entered the forest. An Ogre is a bad-tempered creature that's built like a small European car. Most Ogres are almost as tall as they are broad with muscles built upon muscles which are then built upon more muscles. Their skin is tough and they have a powerful enthusiasm when it comes to axes. Every Ogre owns several axes and always carries at least one on their person, even when they go to bed. They're not known for their academic prowess, nor are they ever called upon to give speeches or solve mathematical equations. The Ogre that lumbered into Eve's forest was named Agrok and he was in a bad mood.

Eve sensed the large creature as soon as he entered the forest and she was having difficulty containing her excitement. She'd seduced and destroyed men, women, gnomes, fairies, humanimals, wizards, witches, and on one rare occasion, a warzgurt, but never an Ogre. The prospect gave her chills. She didn't know what an Ogre woman looked like so it was hard to know what an Ogre desired, but she was excited to find out.

Agrok lumbered through the forest, occasionally knocking down a tree here and there, until he finally fell upon the tranquil pool where the Nymph was perched upon a rock.

"Hello," said Eve. The word sounded guttural and damp.

"Ullo," said the Ogre as he looked upon the slimy stubby little Troll that Eve had turned into.

"Would you like to come over and sit by me?" squelched Eve the Troll.

"No," grinned the Ogre as he hefted his great two-handed axe and cut off the troll's head.

The last thought that passed through Eve's mind was 'why is an Ogre's heart's desire an ugly little troll?' Her head bounced across the lush green landscape and her body slid into the still waters of the pool. In a swift moment the pool dried up and the forest folded in upon itself leaving a confused Ogre standing in the middle of a dry, empty desert.

The Moral of the Fairy Tale:

Use caution when meeting people for the first time. Even if they look exactly like your heart's desire, always remember that appearances can be deceiving.

Or

Ogres love nothing more than to decapitate a Troll. If you happen to be a Troll, you should avoid Ogres at all costs.

4 THE TRAGIC TALE OF THE MESSY WIZARD

Once upon a time in the highest tower of the Wizard's Council Chambers, which was appropriately located in the capital City of Oz, there lived a young wizard called Bartimus Merryweather Elfington III.

Bart, as he was referred to by most, was an apprentice wizard of the third degree. This meant that although he had completed his wizardry schooling, he still had one more degree to pass before being mentored by a member of the noble and prestigious Wizard's Council.

Bart was refraining from attaining such a degree as in his mind 'noble and prestigious' meant 'old, stuffy, and gassy.' Another reason was that to attain the fourth degree he would need to take the Dreaded Fourth Degree Test which was so named due to its dreadfulness. Many third-degree wizards found themselves a little less than alive during the test and by the end of it often discovered, to their dismay, that they were completely dead.

Bart the wizard had no intention of becoming old and gassy and didn't much like the idea of being dead so he occupied himself by being busy doing anything but taking the test.

He kept residence in one of the highest towers in the

Wizard's Council Chambers, which acted as the central nervous system in the world of Thiside by funneling magical energy in all the appropriate directions. Magic, of course, did whatever it damn well pleased but allowed the wizards the perception that they held a certain amount of control over it so as not to worry them.

Bart's residence was a small room with an uncomfortable bed, a sink, a window (through which many students threw themselves in order to escape taking the Dreaded Fourth Degree Test) and an old closet that smelled like old people lived inside of it. The biggest difference between Bart's residence and everyone else's was that he did not clean up after himself. This isn't to say he lacked the ability, but rather he lacked the proper motivation. He was warned by the House Matron, who watched over the apprentice residences, that if he didn't clean up after himself, he would meet a tragic end. She did this daily. Bart's reply would be a hearty laugh.

"I'm warning you," said the Matron, "it'll end badly unless you clean up that room of yours."

"Be gone old lady," said Bart with a laugh, "surely you have other apprentices to bother."

"You shouldn't speak to the Matron like that," said Mergal, a second-degree apprentice, "I heard the Matrons are actually powerful witches who have infiltrated the wizard council and only work here to keep an eye on the apprentices to make sure no sorcerers ever make their way onto the Wizard's Council."

"That's ridiculous Mergal, the last sorcerer died hundreds of years ago and there's absolutely no chance our old Matron is a powerful witch." And with a wave of his hand Bart dismissed the entire notion. "I like my room just the way it is."

"Dirty," said Mergal.

"Yes," said Bart.

"All that junk piled up in the corners so that you can barely move around?"

"It's my comfort zone and I have no intention of changing it."

"What if Matron's right? What if you end up meeting a tragic end?"

"The only way I'm going to meet a tragic end is if I take that dreaded test which I have no intention of doing. No, Mergal, I plan to live a long and healthy life."

Tragically, he was mistaken.

****

Several weeks later as the sun began to set, Bart entered his residence and found the door no longer opened all the way due to the junk piled up behind it. He forced himself inside, knocking over several piles of knick knacks in the process, and flopped down on his bed which was beginning to smell faintly like rotting fruit. He looked around his small room and mentally noted all the objects that were strewn around: a small cage with nothing in it, a collection of glass statutes, a sports racket, crystals, a dead potted plant, two old mattresses, the remains of a chicken, several used pieces of crockery, nine piles of laundry separated into different degrees of filthiness, over a hundred books; mostly never used, four badly charred cauldrons, twelve stuffed animals, one jar of fairy wings, and so on. The air was dense with a number of smells, all of which were fighting for dominance. Bart smiled to himself and began to whistle happily.

****

Outside Bart's residence, the old House Matron walked down the hallway. She stopped outside Bart's door and listened to him whistle.

"I've had it with that lazy little good for nothing," said the Matron to herself and smiled a wicked smile. With a dramatic flourish she cast a spell in front of Bart's door and then continued on her merry way.

****

Bart was drifting off to sleep when he heard the rustling. He sat upright and looked around the dimly lit room. Several damaged scrolls in one corner of the room were shaking. Then his tacky glass statue collection shattered. Several of the stuffed dead animals began to growl and contents of the room began to vibrate in unison.

Bart clutched a pillow to his chest but the pillow refused to stay put and threw itself among the contents of the room. There was a blinding flash of light and the random pieces of junk began to merge together. Slowly the merger began to take form: the ghastly legs were made up of lint, wood, and iron while its midsection was comprised of the stuffed animals. Its massive arms jutted out at odd angles while its eyeless head was nothing but a large angry-looking mouth.

Bart looked on in horror as the entirety of his worldly possessions stood before him looking ghastly.

"Wh-what do you want?" asked Bart, who was trying his best not to sound scared beyond all recognition.

The creature opened its large gaping mouth lined with jagged teeth made of smashed glass statues and then closed it again.

"Oh," said Bart who was reading between the lines.

****

The next day Bart didn't show up for breakfast, skipped lunch, and by dinner time had completely failed to materialize anywhere.

When Mergal and the House Matron entered Bart's residence that night to see what had happened, his room was completely clean. All the junk was gone, the dust had vanished, and Bart was nowhere to be seen.

"He must have left," said Mergal.

The House Matron smiled a small smile and shrugged. "Who knows?"

The Moral of the Fairy Tale:

Dwelling in filth is no way to live your life. Take pride in your surroundings, clean up after yourself, and listen to your elders as they're often smarter than you think.

Or

Beware the garbage monster. He's still out there somewhere.

5 THE CONSEQUENCE OF AN ANGRY FAIRY

Once upon a time there was a Fairy named Alice. As a rule, Fairies fall into three separate categories: The Good, The Bad, and The Simplistic. The Good and Bad are self-explanatory, while the Simplistics, ironically, take a little more explaining.

Good Fairies are good in every possible way; they're bright and colorful, they help people, they assist the Wizards of Oz to usher magic in all the right directions.

Bad Fairies are dark and devious. They lack color in the same way accountants lack a sense of humor. They often travel in packs, they spit, they steal, they use foul language, they're violent, they're twisted, and generally unpleasant to be around.

Simplistic Fairies are too dumb to cause any sort of real harm and often suffer from short life spans as they have a bad habit of flying into things. They're also completely ignorant, so they're rarely seen to be doing any sort of good deed. In the grand scheme of things, the Simplistic Fairies fall squarely in the middle of the Fairy races. While they're unlikely to kill you, they're also as equally unlikely to save your life.

Fairies would generally keep to their own kinds, but on extremely rare occasions a fairy would cross breed across the genetic categories creating a hybrid.

Alice was the production of one such unlikely pairing. She was the result of far too much Jangawanga Juice (highly disorientating, even more so when ingested) on a cold evening between a Simplistic fairy and a Bad fairy. The result was Alice, an extremely angry fairy.

Alice was not bad, nor was she simple. To put it succinctly, she didn't like anything and had no problem telling anything that she didn't like it. The internal sensor that most people have in their heads, the one that tells you that calling your Great Aunt Sally an ugly walrus is a bad idea, just didn't exist for Alice. She would get angry at a moment's notice. Her fuse was shorter than . . . well . . . than a fairy.

When Alice was born, she lived with her Simplistic fairy of a mother who, when Alice was two years old, flew into the side of a castle and died. Alice was adopted by a small village of elderly Good fairies who had a soft spot for the troubled child.

Alice spent a lot of her days shouting. She would shout at her adopted family for not letting her stay out late, she would shout at her teachers that she was smarter than them, she would shout at the wind that it was blowing too hard, or at the flowers because they looked at her funny. Everything angered her.

By the time Alice was nineteen, everyone in her small village knew who she was and chose to stay away from her. Alice maintained a lonely life consisting of one angry encounter after another. Several fairies attempted to counsel her to improve her mood but this only threw her into fits of rage.

****

One fateful day a Good fairy named Shazzle visited the fairy village to bring news from the City of Oz. Unfortunately, the first fairy that Shazzle encountered was Alice.

"Greeting fairy of the North," said Shazzle in the customary fairy greeting. She even fluttered her wings for effect.

Alice sneered at her. "I don't like you," snapped Alice. "You smell strange."

Shazzle was taken aback. "Uh, I'm sorry. My name is Shazzle and I come bearing important news from the City of Oz, I'm an official emissary from—"

"I DON'T CARE WHO YOU ARE!" shouted Alice. "AND I DON'T LIKE YOUR NAME, AND I ESPECIALLY DON'T LIKE THE CITY OF OZ."

Shazzle began to look scared. This too angered Alice. "Uh, I'm sorry," stuttered Shazzle, "it's important though that—"

"YOU'RE UGLY!"

"I'm uh…sorry? I don't underst—"

"GET OUT! GET OUT OF MY VILLAGE SHNIZZLE!"

"Shazzle," whimpered Shazzle.

"I HATE YOUR HAIR," yelled Alice into Shazzle's face, "GET OUUUUTTTTTT!" she shouted until she turned such a fierce color of red that it looked like she might explode.

Tiny tears streaked down Shazzle's face and she flew off as fast as she could until she was nothing but a tiny blur in the distance.

Unfortunately for Alice's village, the important news was that a new road was about to be magically laid right through their area. This would cause the complete destruction of their village, but the City of Oz had arranged for them to be moved to a new village that had been specially built for them. As the news was never relayed, the fairies of the village were shocked two days later when a destructive wave of magic flattened their village and a second wave of magic built a brand-new shiny road over the top of it. No fairies were killed or even hurt, but they were instantaneously homeless. A meeting was called and even Alice showed up in case someone needed shouting at.

"Why would no one tell us about this?" asked one old fairy.

"Surely the Wizards of Oz would have notified us, it must be some sort of mistake?" added another.

An elderly fairy named Frander said "They normally send an emissary for these sorts of things."

"Ohhh that!" said Alice with a roll of her eyes. "There was some whosey-watzit here a couple of days ago but she made me angry and then she flew off. I didn't like her very much."

The entire fairy village stared at her in shocked disbelief.

The now homeless fairies agreed to sleep in the branches of a large tree for the night and would decide the best course of action the next morning. The decision made Alice angry and she shouted about it.

****

The next morning when Alice awoke, everyone had gone. A single tiny note had been tied to her wrist. It read:

Dear Alice,

You're extremely angry and generally unpleasant to be around. We've decided to move on without you. Good luck.

Sincerely,

Everyone

Not surprisingly this made Alice angry. She shouted at anything that would (or couldn't) listen for most of the morning before finally flying off in a fit of rage. She ended up on the northern edge of the Dark Forest where all manner of sinister creatures dwelled. Alice didn't care about the creatures, she just wanted someone else to be angry at. She flew down into a small clearing in the forest to rest her wings.

Two saucer sized red eyes blinked at her from the darkness.

"What are you?" snapped Alice.

The large red eyes blinked again and then they moved forward emerging from the shadows to reveal itself as a Grodlic. Grodlics were rare in Thiside but not because they were hunted or endangered. They were rare because Grodlics didn't like their own kind which made breeding difficult. They were unfriendly creatures with a scaly blue body, four legs, six arms, several sets of sharp claws, and a large head containing two red eyes and a gaping mouth that looked distinctly pointy and sharp. A Grodlic is best described as a cross between a very ugly, frozen alligator, and a Shetland pony with several extra limbs.

The Grodlic sniffed at Alice and this made her angry.

"Don't sniff me!" screeched Alice. She watched as the Grodlic shrank closer to the ground and began to shake slightly. This made Alice angrier. "You're a very ugly creature!" she shouted, "I've been blamed for the destruction of my village, I've been abandoned by my people, and I'm not in a good mood!"

The Grodlic tilted its head sideways and began to whimper. Alice's rage reached a crescendo and she threw her anger from the entire day into her tiny fairy voice.

"YOU ARE A COWARDLY CREATURE AND I HAAAATTTEE YOOUUUU!!" she shouted.

The Grodlic began to cry as it shook with apparent fear; massive tears flowed from its oversized red eyes.

Alice shook her head in disgust and was about to fly away when the Grodlic's tongue flicked out and wrapped itself firmly around Alice's tiny fairy body, then snapped back into its gaping jaws full of shiny, sharp teeth.

Its mouth snapped closed with a 'crunch' followed by a

satisfied 'gulp'.

The Grodlic stopped shaking, scratched its rear end with one if it's six arms, and disappeared into the dark forest.

The Moral of the Fairy Tale:

Think before you speak and never express yourself through anger. Not only will it cause problems throughout your life but it will also render you sad and lonely . . . and possibly eaten alive.

Or

If you find yourself alone with a Grodlic and it starts to cry and look scared, RUN! They're only doing that to lead you into a false sense of security before eating you.

6 THE LAST SORCERER

Once upon a time, a very long time ago, in the world of Thiside there lived the last of the great Sorcerers. As his inevitable death loomed ever closer, he was wrought with despair. As the last of his line the sorcerer had yet to leave his mark on the world. Those that preceded him had created amazing things, built cities from an acorn, created new creatures and, in one unique case, invented the toilet seat (which was never utilized for its true purpose, but was instead implemented for more practical application; stopping one's buttocks from touching the distasteful rim around a toilet bowl).

And then it occurred to him. He realized what his contribution to the world should be: he would create the first ever perfect woman. It is widely known in Thiside that Sorcerers operate on a completely different wave length from all other magical entities. They are infinitely more powerful than a wizard or magi, and rather than creating spells they are able to manipulate the magical energy around them in the same way that a potter manipulates clay.

The Sorcerer waited for the perfect day when the clouds were just the right shade of grey and the wind would whip his bright red robes around his body in a dramatic fashion. He packed his singular supply and set out from his tiny cottage in the North Western region at the foot of the Grimm Mountains and began his long climb to the Peak of Magical Significance (so named due to its magical significance).

At the ripe old age of three-hundred and seventy-six, the Sorcerer didn't move all that fast and the sun was beginning to set with a flourish as he finally crested the peak. The Peak of Magical Significance, which was conveniently flat on top allowing any number of magical ceremonies, spells, and songs to be performed, crackled with raw energy. The sky began to darken and the clouds loomed heavily above him as he removed a bright green rock from his bag and placed it in the center of the open area. The magical energy skittered and jumped toward the rock causing it to glow and lightning shot across the sky as if to prove a point.

The Sorcerer smiled at the atmospheric discharge of magic and raw power, felt it flow through his body, and tickle his toes. He raised both his hands in the air as the wind whipped around him, opened his mouth . . . and then closed it again.

He knew what he wanted to do but was unsure where to start. Sorcerers and wizards didn't really consort with females other than witches who were often distasteful. This was silly. He was an all-powerful Sorcerer with the elements at his command. He raised his arms again, lightning ripped the sky in half, he opened his mouth and began:

"Alright here we go then. I'm going to start with the body. Not too tall of course, classy but not a bone rack, a little curvy but not so much that she looks like she's bent at all the wrong angles."

The green rock began to luminescently throb and from the essence of nothingness the Sorcerer called into existence the skeletal frame of a woman floating in mid-air.

Muscle and sinew threaded its way out of the air and began to wrap itself around the bones creating the physical presence of a body. The wind thrashed across the mountain top and the Sorcerer almost lost his pointy hat.

He waved his hands for dramatic emphasis and then paused to scratch his head. The female body made only of bone and muscle rotated slowly and the wind abruptly dropped.

"What kind of skin should she have?" said the Sorcerer to no one in particular.

He seemed to remember his mother having very tanned skin but that never seemed practical to him. The perfect woman should be easy to find at all times.

"I'll make her pale so she'll stand out and can be easily located at all times."

He threw his hands into the air and the wind began to rush and swirl once again as he called into action the most physical of elements and skin began to grow over the woman's body. With his right hand the Sorcerer reached up and plucked a star from the darkening sky and flung it at the woman's empty eye sockets. The woman blinked once to reveal grayish green eyes, like the depths of the ocean on a cloudy day with the sparkle of the stars concealed within.

He summoned the mental energy of the closest populated city and funneled it directly into the woman to give her a mind of her own. This was his last great mistake.

What he had failed to do was research who lived in the closest populated city. As a cruel twist of fate, the closest populated city was actually more of a settlement populated entirely by females. The four hundred or so women were an angry bunch who had joined together to fight the disease that they classified as 'man'. This radical group did not believe in the notion that a woman needed a man to justify her existence and regarded the male gender as a problem that had no viable answer. The settlement had come to be known by the surrounding area as Feminisity.

No one knew why, it just seemed to fit. It was from the collective minds of the residents of Feminisity that the Sorcerer drew the thoughts and beliefs and focused them into his creation.

The wind was now swirling around the mountain like a tornado as the Sorcerer called upon all the elements to finish what he had begun.

"Hair!" he shouted to the wind. "Make it red! Make it as red as the . . . uh . . . the . . . something very red!"

This part he was most proud of. Red hair did not exist in the world of Thiside. There was auburn and brown, blonde and black, and in rare cases an off shade of blue, but not one individual in Thiside had red hair and the Sorcerer had always wondered what it would look like.

The most beautiful red hair sprouted from his subject, and grew to flow down her back. The wind slowed and the Sorcerer looked upon his creation. She glided to the ground and stared out through vacant eyes.

"Yes, very nice," said the Sorcerer, "the perfect woman! I've done it! They said it couldn't be done, but I've done it! I'll call her a 'red head', what a lovely name and she will be the sweetest kindest creature to ever walk the earth."

The Sorcerer lowered his hands and snapped his fingers a couple of times.

"Time for you to awaken my beloved creature."

The woman's eyes took on a look of bewilderment as she blinked a few times and looked carefully at the Sorcerer and around at her surroundings. Her face was the picture of innocence. She looked down at her body and realized she was naked, then back at the old man who was grinning at her.

'Why am I naked?' she thought. 'Why is he grinning at me? What does he want?'

The woman looked again at herself and back at the man and then something happened. Something ingrained in her very short existence bubbled to the surface, a sort of collective negative opinion formed from the minds of four hundred angry women.

The Sorcerer beckoned to her in a welcoming motion. "That's right my dear, come to me now, I am your creat—"

The woman screamed a shrill scream that ricocheted across the peaks of the Grimm Mountains. A look of rage and indignation swept across her face as she searched for a weapon. Seeing the glowing green rock, she grabbed it and flung it at the Sorcerer with all her might striking the old man in the head causing him to stagger backwards and off the edge of the cliff.

The woman, still angry, walked to the edge and watched with satisfaction as the last living Sorcerer bounced down the side of the mountain to his timely death with all the dexterity of an uncoordinated brick.

The first ever 'red head' in existence gave a satisfied 'humph' and disappeared into the night to wreak havoc on an unsuspecting world.

The Moral of the Fairy Tale:

Do not dabble in that which you don't understand and have absolutely no capacity to comprehend. Instead, just stick to what you know.

Or

Be wary of red headed women. While their scarcity and magical properties make them desirable, their anger is powerful enough to make the fiercest of creatures pee themselves.

ABOUT THE AUTHOR

Andrew Buckley is a traditionally published author of rather silly, yet enjoyable fiction for all ages. As an ex-pat Brit living in Canada, Andrew is a passionate nerd, movie-lover, avid reader, comic book geek, public speaker, podcaster, and dances a mean cha-cha. He's also the co-founder and instructor at Wordsmith Academy, an online writing school.